AND THAT'S WHEN I GET MY CRYSTAL-CLEAR IDEA

I will borrow six of my dad's crystals—only six!—from his office this very minute, and sneak them up to my room.

Then tomorrow, Tuesday, I will ask Ms. Sanchez if I can show everyone the crystals, and talk—okay brag—about them, and she will say yes, because crystals are so scientific and beautiful. Everyone in my class will be totally AMAZED and IMPRESSED, and it will be the best Tuesday I ever had in my life. I might even get extra credit!

Then I will take all the crystals home tomorrow afternoon and sneak them back onto the shelf so they will be there when he gets home.

There is *no way* this plan can go wrong!

OTHER BOOKS YOU MAY ENJOY

Only Emma	Sally Warner/Jamie Harper
Super Emma	Sally Warner/Jamie Harper
Ellray Jakes Is <u>Not</u> a Chicken	Sally Warner/Jamie Harper
George Brown, Class Clown: Super Burp	Nancy Krulik/ Aaron Blecha
George Brown, Class Clown: Trouble Magnet	Nancy Krulik/ Aaron Blecha
Friendship According to Humphrey	Betty G. Birney
Surprises According to Humphrey	Betty G. Birney
The World According to Humphrey	Betty G. Birney
Horrible Harry Bugs the Three Bears	Suzy Kline/ Frank Remkiewicz
Horrible Harry Goes Cuckoo	Suzy Kline/Amy Wummer
Horrible Harry and the Green Slime	Suzy Kline/ Frank Remkiewicz
Horrible Harry and the Secret Treasure	Suzy Kline/Amy Wummer

EllRay Jakes
is a Rock Star!

BY **Sally Warner**

ILLUSTRATED BY
Jamie Harper

PUFFIN BOOKS
An Imprint of Penguin Group (USA) Inc.

PUFFIN BOOKS
Published by the Penguin Group
Penguin Young Readers Group, 345 Hudson Street, New York, New York 10014, U.S.A.
Penguin Group (Canada), 90 Eglinton Avenue East, Suite 700, Toronto, Ontario, Canada M4P 2Y3
(a division of Pearson Penguin Canada Inc.)
Penguin Books Ltd, 80 Strand, London WC2R 0RL, England
Penguin Ireland, 25 St Stephen's Green, Dublin 2, Ireland (a division of Penguin Books Ltd)
Penguin Group (Australia), 250 Camberwell Road, Camberwell, Victoria 3124, Australia
(a division of Pearson Australia Group Pty Ltd)
Penguin Books India Pvt Ltd, 11 Community Centre, Panchsheel Park, New Delhi - 110 017, India
Penguin Group (NZ), 67 Apollo Drive, Rosedale, Auckland 0632, New Zealand
(a division of Pearson New Zealand Ltd.)
Penguin Books (South Africa) (Pty) Ltd, 24 Sturdee Avenue,
Rosebank, Johannesburg 2196, South Africa

Registered Offices: Penguin Books Ltd, 80 Strand, London WC2R 0RL, England

First published in the United States of America by Viking,
a division of Penguin Young Readers Group, 2011
Published by Puffin Books, a division of Penguin Young Readers Group, 2012

5 7 9 10 8 6 4

THE LIBRARY OF CONGRESS HAS CATALOGED THE VIKING EDITION AS FOLLOWS:
Warner, Sally.
EllRay Jakes is a rock star / by Sally Warner ; illustrated by Jamie Harper.
p. cm.
Summary: Eight-year-old EllRay Jakes decides to "borrow" his father's crystals to impress
his classmates, but his plan to return the crystals before his father notices goes awry.
ISBN: 978-0-670-01158-2 (hc)
[1. Behavior—Fiction. 2. Bullies—Fiction. 3. Schools—Fiction.
4. Family life—California —Fiction. 5. African Americans—Fiction. 6. California—Fiction.]
I. Harper, Jamie, ill. II. Title.
Pz7.W24644Els 2011
[Fic]—dc22 2011009182

Puffin Books ISBN 978-0-14-241989-2

Book design by Nancy Brennan
Text set in ITC Century

Printed in the United States of America

For Ben Haworth —S.W.

For Henry —J.H.

CONTENTS

⤫ ⤫ ⤫

TALLER

"I grew an inch last weekend," my friend Kevin McKinley announces at lunch on Friday, smiling like it's no big deal. But it is.

Kevin is brown like me, but already he is **TALLER** than I am, so him growing another inch does not seem fair.

Why can't nature make things come out even? I don't get it.

It is Valentine's Day in exactly one week, which means this is almost the middle of February. Just about every kid in Ms. Sanchez's third grade class is outside, including me, because it is the first sunny day we have had in a long time. Even the birds are having fun. Crows are turning circles in the air.

"No, you did not grow an inch in one weekend," Cynthia Harbison says, basically calling Kevin a liar. **"THAT'S IMPOSSIBLE."**

Everyone holds their breath when Cynthia says something like this. She's usually right, and she likes to boss people around. But mostly, she bosses the girls—especially Emma McGraw and Annie Pat Masterson.

Cynthia's dad has a really cool car, though. It's an Audi. And she's very neat, if you like that kind of thing, which I do not.

"It is not impossible to grow that fast," Corey Robinson says, defending Kevin. He is usually pretty quiet, and he has freckles on his face. Corey smells like chlorine all the time.

Corey is a champion swimmer, but he's not that tall. He's a pretty cool guy. In fact, he's *very* cool. He doesn't threaten to beat me up the way Jared Matthews and his best friend and faithful robot Stanley Washington used to do.

Jared is widely known as the meanest kid in our class. He is absent today.

"Yeah," I chime in, because Kevin's also my

friend. "Maybe he hung upside-down all day long both days, and his legs stretched."

As I say the words, I wonder why I didn't think of this first, because I am the shortest kid—including all the girls!—in our class at Oak Glen Primary School in Oak Glen, California, USA.

Hanging upside-down! It's worth a shot, because:

1. I have already tried drinking so much milk that it almost comes out of my nose when I laugh.

2. And I have tried sleeping straight, not curled up like the shrimp that I am.

3. And I have tried "thinking positive," which is something my dad always recommends. He is a champion positive thinker, unlike my mom, who is a worrywart. She also wants to be a writer of fantasy books for grown-ups, which is why my little sister Alfleta—"Alfie"—and I have such weird names.

My real name is Lancelot Raymond Jakes, in case you didn't know. But please, *please*, just call me EllRay.

My dad's name is Dr. Warren Jakes, and he teaches geology at a college in San Diego. He is very smart, and he is *bigger* than normal-sized, so maybe there is still hope for me.

"I believe you, Kevin," Emma says, daring to argue with Cynthia. "But how do you know you grew an inch?"

"Because my mom marked it on the wall," Kevin tells her—and everyone. "And the last time she did that, I was a whole inch shorter."

"When was that?" Emma asks.

"Last summer," Kevin says. "On the Fourth of July."

Cynthia snickers behind her hand. "Kevin's mom writes on the wall! That's so messy," she says to Fiona McNulty, who is the shyest girl in our class. Fiona has weak ankles, she tells us way too often.

Fiona really admires Cynthia, though. "Yeah. Writing on the wall is so messy," she says, sounding like an echo.

Kevin scowls. "You better not be making fun of my mom," he says in a low and scary voice.

And he's right to say that, because kids can say any bad thing they want about another kid, if they have the nerve, but parents are off-limits.

Also sisters and brothers, unless the kid officially hates them.

Already-tall Stanley Washington frowns and

pushes up his glasses higher on his nose. "But that doesn't make any sense," he says, as if he has been dividing numbers in his head.

"You grew an inch since *last summer*, Kevin," Krysten—"Kry"—Rodriguez says, backing Stanley up. "Not over the weekend."

Kry is very pretty, and she's also good at math and at figuring things out.

"Well, I know *that*," Kevin says. He would be looking mad if anyone else had said what Kry did, but everybody in my class likes Kry.

She's another positive thinker.

"That's what I meant to say the whole time," Kevin continues. "Only somebody interrupted me."

We all turn to look at Cynthia, but Cynthia just shrugs. "Well, who even cares?" she says, straightening the plastic hoop she wears to hold her hair back from her face. "Anyway," she adds like she is making perfect sense, "my dad's taller than Kevin's dad."

That doesn't break the rule about not criticizing parents, but it comes pretty close. We think about it for a while.

"What does that have to do with anything?" Corey finally asks.

"I'm just saying," Cynthia says, satisfied, and Fiona gives her an admiring smile.

"Well, who even cares who's taller?" Stanley says. "Because Jared's dad has a lot cooler stuff than *all* your dads. In fact, he got a brand-new ATV just last week. It's red, and it has flame decals all over it."

"ATV" stands for "All-Terrain Vehicle," and you can ride them *fast* in the desert or at the beach. Lots of places. You don't even need roads.

My dad would probably never buy an ATV, though, because he likes to protect the environment, I guess mostly because the environment has a lot of rocks in it.

I like the environment, too, but I really want to ride in that ATV with the flames.

"Jared's dad might have cooler stuff," Kevin says, defending his father, "but I'll bet my dad has a ton more *money* than him. Because he doesn't spend it all on ATVs, that's why. He saves it."

The girls are looking uncomfortable by now, but none of them walks away.

"Jared's dad has a lot of money, too," Stanley argues. "He wears solid gold jewelry and everything."

And I am thinking two things. First, Stanley is making Mr. Matthews sound like an ATV-driving rap star, if there is such a thing, only he's not. Mr. Matthews is just a regular dad—if you can have someone extreme like Jared for your kid and still be regular.

Second, how did we end up talking about whose dad makes the most money? We were talking about tallness! Then we were talking about *stuff*. How did this lunch period turn into a bragging contest about whose family is the richest— when so many other kids' families are having money troubles?

Maybe even kids here at Oak Glen Primary School.

I already know I could never win this contest, because college professors like my dad don't make a ton of money. Not to hear him tell it. Not compared to some people.

And people who want to write fantasy books for grown-ups make even less.

So how can I compete?

What do *I* have to brag about?

I have to **FIND SOMETHING!**

GETTING READY FOR VALENTINE'S DAY

"Psst," Emma whispers later that day. "Are you done with the red marker?"

"Yeah," I say gloomily, snapping the lid on and handing it over. I was drawing a huge ladybug with stingers and fangs, but whatever.

"Isn't this *so much fun?*" she asks.

Valentine's Day is a huge deal at Oak Glen Primary School—for the girls, anyway.

All the boys in school say they hate it, not counting the ones in kindergarten—but I think kindergarten boys only like Valentine's Day because of the treats.

In the third grade, it's different. But at least Valentine's Day is a change, because other than that, nothing interesting happens at school between Christmas vacation and spring break.

At our school, nobody worries about kids' feelings getting hurt because they didn't get enough valentines, which is the way it used to be in the olden days, my mom says. Our school has strict rules about giving people valentines.

1. If you send a valentine to one kid in your class, you have to send valentines to everyone. Even girls-to-girls and boys-to-boys, which is just embarrassing. But you can send funny ones if you want. Funny, but not too gross.
2. Also, the valentines can't have candy or glitter or confetti in them, because of the custodian's temper.
3. And you can't open your cards until the school day is almost over.

But getting ready for Valentine's Day is a pain, because I have to figure out what kind of valentines I am going to send—to the kids in my class, to Ms.

Sanchez, and to my mom and my little sister.

Not to my dad, of course. That's just not us.

Alfie has already informed me that a card to her is *required*, and it had better be good.

We have been making valentines in class today, because Friday is art day. Ms. Sanchez is probably relieved that Valentine's Day is coming, because she can never figure out what to do when we have art. She gloms on to any theme she can: Thanksgiving, President's Day, Arbor Day, you name it. We cover all the Days.

Today is the last Friday we have to work on our cards, though, because like I said, Valentine's Day is in exactly one week.

"I'm making mine all the same, so I'll finish first. I'll win," Stanley tells us. He has a stack of folded construction paper pieces in front of him, and he is scrawling a heart on the outside of each one with a black marker, and a question mark on the inside. He's like a cartoon guy working in a factory, he's going so fast.

By the way, the question mark is supposed to stand for "Guess who?" That's a good way to get around actually signing your name on a valentine.

Just a hint!

"It's not a contest, *Stanley*," Annie Pat Masterson says, drawing the world's fanciest seahorse on one of her cards. Annie Pat is Emma's best friend, and she always fixes her red hair in two pigtails that look like highway warning cones.

"Yeah," Emma says.

"I think everything's a contest," Cynthia argues, not looking up from the card she is working on. "The clothes you wear, how cute your hair is, what you bring for lunch, how late you get to stay up, what your grades are. Only it's different contests

for different people. Like, today, my valentines are in the *cute* contest, and I'm winning."

And she draws another unicorn.

Yaw-w-w-n.

Ms. Sanchez is at the end of the table showing Kry how to fold a piece of paper to cut out a perfect heart, so she doesn't hear what Cynthia is saying.

Beside Cynthia, Fiona nods to show how much she agrees with her.

The boys are just listening, because drawing is hard enough, isn't it? You can't talk at the same time.

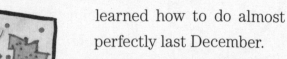

Well, Stanley can, but look at his valentines.

Kevin is drawing UFOs, and Corey is drawing Christmas trees, because that's what he learned how to do almost perfectly last December.

But he's putting hearts on them.

"That doesn't make any sense," Emma tells Cynthia. "Because how do you know who else is in the same contest as you?"

"You just know, that's all," Cynthia tells her, smiling in a superior way. "At least I do. I know when I'm winning. Like now," she adds, looking at the valentine Emma is working on as if someone just blew their nose on it.

"Yours is good, Emma," Annie Pat says, defending her friend's drawing of a frog sitting on a lily pad. Or a green meatball with eyes, sitting on a plate. "It's *cute*. Here," she adds. "Use my pink marker. It smells like cherries."

"I'll take that," Cynthia says, snatching the pink marker from Annie Pat's hand in mid-air. "I need it first. Ahhh," she says, sniffing in the cherry smell like she wants to use it all up.

"That's okay," Emma says to Annie Pat, whose dark blue eyes are looking angry. Annie Pat is quiet, but she can be dangerous. "I don't even need pink for a frog," Emma says. "And look," she adds in a whisper, jerking her head toward Cynthia, who is snuffling the marker again.

There is a bright pink dot on the end of Cynthia's stuck-up nose, where she sniffed the marker too close.

It looks like a great big measle!

Annie Pat bites back a smile, and so do Corey, Stanley, and I.

And Fiona's afraid to say anything to Cynthia,

because she and Cynthia aren't exactly equal. Cynthia's already won that contest.

"Now, today is even more fun than before," Emma says, bending low over her frog. Or green meatball. Whatever it is.

"Finish up, people," Ms. Sanchez calls out, sounding happy. I guess she's proud of the perfect heart she just cut out.

And so we do. Finish up, I mean.

✳ **3** ✳

STRAYING FROM THE TOPIC

"Where's Dad?" I ask my mom when Alfie and I sit down to dinner that night—at six o'clock, as usual.

"Oh, EllRay," Mom says, carrying a bowl of spaghetti to the table. "Don't you ever listen to me? I told you this morning. He's speaking at a conference in Utah over the weekend, and then going hiking with a buddy. He'll be home late Tuesday."

"He went to Utah?" Alfie says, almost squawking the question. "Without *me*?"

"Why? What would you do in Utah?" I ask my little sister. "We don't know anyone there."

"I'd have fun, that's what," Alfie says, staring hard at the spaghetti bowl. "I always have fun. Do I have to eat salad too, or can I just eat this?" she asks my mom. "I had carrot sticks for lunch," she reminds her.

Alfie is an optimist, which means she is another positive thinker. She's only four, exactly half my age, so she hasn't had that much experience with life yet.

"You have to eat salad too," Mom tells her.

"Okay," Alfie says. "But don't put anything weird on it. *Please*," she adds quickly, seeing the look on our mother's face.

Mom frowns. "Just because it's Friday night and your father is away for the weekend," she says, "that doesn't mean important things such as manners can go flying out the window."

"Yeah, *EllWay*," Alfie says, trying to kick me under the table. That's Alfie-speak for EllRay.

"She was talking to *you*," I tell her, moving my legs away.

"I'm talking to both of you," Mom says, putting some bare salad in a little bowl for Alfie, and then tossing the rest of the torn-up lettuce with salad dressing. "There," she says, sitting down. "You may begin."

And the three of us are quiet for a few minutes as we slurp up our noodles.

Well, my mother doesn't slurp, she winds the noodles around her fork. But that's hard. Only grown-ups can do it.

I clear my throat, because I have something important to say—and my dad being gone means that this is the perfect time to say it. "We should get an ATV," I say, looking at my plate. I try to sound like an ATV is something our family obviously needs, only we have forgotten to buy one before now.

"Yeah," Alfie agrees. "And we should put it in my room so I can watch anything I want. In the middle of the night, even."

Mom dabs at her lips with her napkin, which doesn't even have any spaghetti sauce marks on it, even though we have been eating for almost five minutes. She smiles. "I don't really see that happening, sweetie," she says to Alfie. "You watch enough TV as it is."

"Not a *TV*," I say quickly, before Alfie can start arguing. "An ATV. That's an All-Terrain Vehicle."

"Boo," Alfie murmurs, losing interest.

"I know what an ATV is, EllRay," my mom tells me. "And I can't really see your father buying one, can you?"

"Yes, I definitely can," I say. "It would be useful when we're collecting rocks. You can have an ATV and still love the environment, you know."

"But don't you think your father's more likely to spend any extra money we might have paying bills, or put it into your college savings accounts?" she asks me. "Or even into our retirement fund?" she adds, not looking very hopeful.

Alfie looks up. "Only grandmas and grandpas

retire," she informs us. "They're old. And you're not old, Mommy. Not *that* old."

Alfie's kissing up—for no reason. Just to keep in practice, I guess.

"Well, thank you, Miss Alfie," Mom says. "But your daddy and I will be old, someday."

Alfie looks at her, horrified. "No," she says. "I don't want—"

"An *ATV*," I interrupt, because we are straying from the topic, as Ms. Sanchez so often tells us. "For the desert and the mountains and the beach. Lots of people have them."

"Name one," my mom challenges me.

"Jared's dad," I tell her.

"Ahhh."

She says it like that because Jared and I have had some problems in the past.

In the past few weeks, even.

I can tell my mom thinks I'm jealous of Jared and his ATV. Which I am, a little.

"Jared's lucky," Alfie says sadly, speaking to her last few noodles.

"You're telling me," I mutter.

"Well," Mom says, "I'll pass the suggestion along to your father when he gets home, EllRay."

"How about asking him when he calls tonight?" I suggest—because that way, my dad will have a chance to get used to the idea.

Maybe he won't say no right away, at least.

"If I get the chance," Mom promises. "But don't get your hopes up. And finish your delicious salad."

4

KIND OF CRAZY

"Hi, Dad?" I say later that night when my mom hands me the phone. Alfie has already gone to bed, or she'd be hogging the whole conversation.

"Hello, son," my father says. His voice does not sound very far away, which makes me feel nervous because of what I am about to suggest.

"How's the conference going?" I say, wanting to be polite before asking for an ATV when it's not even Christmas or my birthday—and when I can't even drive yet.

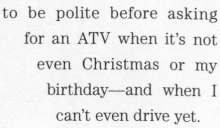

"It's going fine," Dad tells me. "I'm presenting my paper tomorrow morning."

"Well, I don't want to bother you," I say, still being super polite. "I just thought maybe we should buy an ATV when you get home. With flames."

I think saying "we" was a good idea, and so was saying the whole thing really fast.

"Flames?" my dad says, as if he has just now started paying attention to what I am saying. "What's this about flames?"

"*Pretend* flames," I say quickly, before he calls the fire department long distance. "They're decals, really. On the sides of our new ATV."

"What new ATV?" Dad asks, sounding confused.

"The one you should buy when you get home," I tell him patiently. "For driving in the desert when we're collecting rocks."

"Why?" my dad asks, shuffling some papers. I can hear him do it!

"You're not even paying attention," I complain.

"Yes I am," my dad says. "You want me to buy a new ATV when we already have a perfectly good Jeep. A classic. It's practically vintage, son."

"That just means old," I tell him. "And our Jeep doesn't have any flames on it. It's rusty, too."

"We can spray-paint some flames on," Dad says, laughing. "Just you and I, EllRay."

"*Really*?" I say, because this sounds like a very un-Dad activity.

"Sure," my dad says. "Why not? If we're careful, and wear masks while we're spraying."

Being careful and wearing a mask is not the way *I* would spray-paint flames on a Jeep, if I had a choice, but it's better than nothing. "And not Alfie?" I ask.

"Not a chance, if you can keep it under your hat," Dad says. This means I should keep my mouth shut and not go blabbing anything about spray paint to my little sister. "This is going to be fun, EllRay," my dad says, like I need telling. "We'll go shopping for the paint when I get home, and you can choose the colors. How does that sound?"

"Good," I say, suddenly feeling like I don't even know my own father. We've hardly ever done anything like this before, that's why. Something alone, and kind of crazy, just to make me happy. "Thanks," I mumble into the phone.

"You're welcome, son," Dad says.

"'Night," I tell him.

"Good night, EllRay. And sleep tight," my dad says.

So, that's good, I think, hanging up the phone.

But I still don't have anything big to brag about.

✳ 5 ✳

MY CRYSTAL-CLEAR IDEA

On Monday night before bed, as my mom is giving Alfie her usual three-towel bath, I wander into Dad's home office to look around—because I kind of miss him.

Also, I usually don't get to go in there unless I'm in trouble.

Even though almost anyone would think that being a geology professor is boring, my dad's office is pretty cool. The wall opposite his desk is completely covered with wood shelves that are so narrow an apple would feel fat sitting there. All my dad's favorite small rock specimens are on these shelves, and each one is carefully labeled. The rocks are from all over the world—Asia, South America, North America—and he collected each specimen himself.

My dad has been *everywhere*.

My favorite shelves are the ones nearest the window, because those hold the crystals. Dad put the crystals there so that sunlight will shine on them first thing in the morning. He says it's a nice way to start the day.

Crystals grow on or in rocks, and they are like diamonds, only better—because they're much bigger, and they come in so many different colors: blue, green, red, orange, and yellow. Even the gray and brown crystals are awesome, not to mention the clear ones that are like ice that never melts.

And crystals look like somebody carved them, only they grew that way. Nature was the carver.

But my dad was the guy who collected them, and he has a story for each one.

My dad's rock specimens are his life scrapbook, practically.

I just wish some of the kids in my class could see them. Maybe then they'd stop bragging about their dads' ATVs, and their money, and their solid gold jewelry, and how everything's a contest that they are winning.

The kids in my class would see how **AWESOME** my dad's crystals are.

And I would win.

That's when I get my crystal-clear idea.

I will borrow six of my dad's crystals—only six!—from his office this very minute, and sneak them up to my room. Then I'll put each crystal in its very own white tube sock for protection, so they won't get knocked around inside my backpack when I take them to school tomorrow.

But before that, I'll spread out the other crystals on my dad's shelf so Mom won't see any empty places in case she goes into the office before he gets home late tomorrow night.

Then tomorrow, Tuesday, I will ask Ms. Sanchez if I can show everyone the crystals, and talk—okay, brag—about them, and she will say yes, because

crystals are so scientific and beautiful. Everyone in my class will be totally **AMAZED** and **IMPRESSED**, and it will be the best Tuesday I ever had in my life. I might even get extra credit!

Then I will take all the crystals home tomorrow afternoon and sneak them back onto the shelf so they will be there when he gets home. He will never know that six of his crystals took a field trip to Oak Glen Elementary School—to make both him and me look good.

There is *no way* this plan can go wrong!

RARE AND VALUABLE

I walk to the front of the class on Tuesday afternoon. I am holding my backpack against my chest with very cold hands.

"Aren't we a little old for show-and-tell?" Cynthia asks in her most sarcastic voice.

"We're never too old to learn something new," Ms. Sanchez says. "And EllRay has some truly beautiful things to show us. Mr. Jakes?" she says, pretending to introduce me to the class.

"Hi," I mumble. I feel very embarrassed and shy, even though I know secret stuff about almost all the kids sitting in front of me:

1. How Jared Matthews sometimes sleeps with masking tape on his hair to make it lie flat.
2. How Stanley Washington has already started saving up for contact lenses.

3. How Emma McGraw sometimes wishes she had a baby brother or sister, or at least a pet.

4. How Fiona McNulty doesn't really have weak ankles, even though she says she does.

"Hi," a couple of kids say, curious in advance.

"What do you have to share with us?" Ms. Sanchez asks, trying to give me a hint about what to say next.

But I have it all planned—and rehearsed. I plunk my backpack on Ms. Sanchez's desk and unzip it. "I brought six rare and valuable crystals to show you today," I say, and I pull out the six bulging tube socks. I set the socks in a straight line on the desk.

"Those are just boys' socks," Cynthia announces to the class. "And they aren't rare *or* valuable. They're smelly, that's all."

"Would you care to wait out in the hall while we listen to what EllRay has to say, Miss Harbison?" Ms. Sanchez asks in her iciest voice.

"Sorry," Cynthia mutters, shooting me a dirty look.

"Okay," I tell everyone. "I brought six **RARE** and **VALUABLE** crystals that my dad went all around the world to find for his collection. He's in Utah right now, in fact, doing important stuff. And here's the first crystal," I say, carefully shaking it out of its sock, which I labeled last night with a permanent marker.

"OOH," a couple of girls in the front row say, staring at the crystal.

"This is called a topaz," I say, holding it up. It

looks like see-through gold, even though topazes are often brown. This topaz's sides are so perfectly smooth that they look like someone polished them. "It's from Brazil, in South America," I tell everyone. "And it got this way all by itself."

"No way," Jared cough-says in the back row.

"Way," I say coolly. "And next is another crystal from Brazil. It's called a tourmaline." And I hold up a beautiful crystal that looks like a piece of the sky, it is so clear and blue. "Tourmalines are also found in some places in the USA, but like I said, my dad found this one in Brazil. Which is where the Amazon River is," I add, inspired. "With piranhas and everything. Not to mention all the snakes."

Fiona McNulty shudders, probably thinking about those piranhas and snakes. The kids in my class are quiet now, and they are staring at the last four tube socks with hungry eyes. They never knew crystals were this cool! They never knew *I* was this cool. Or my dad.

"And here is an aquamarine crystal," I say, holding a blue-green crystal up to the light. It looks like solid swimming pool water. "This crystal is from Pakistan, which is right next to India. Pakistan is pretty dangerous now because of the politics. And it was probably dangerous when my dad went there, too, but he didn't even care!"

I sneak a peek at Jared. He looks impressed by my dad's bravery.

A little, anyway.

Ms. Sanchez taps at her watch, which means that I should hurry up.

"And my number four crystal is called a garnet," I say, holding up a dark red crystal formation.

"Ooh," the girls in the front row say again.

"This crystal is from India, where there are Indians," I tell everyone. "But not the same kind of Indians as in our country, where they are called Native Americans."

Ms. Sanchez should be giving me even *more* extra credit for this, I think—because it's history, geography, and science—all at the same time!

"And my number five crystal is called smoky quartz," I say, holding up a clear gray formation that looks like a wizard could turn it into a crystal ball that really works, if he wanted to. "It's from Nevada, which is only one state away from here," I say. "And I've gone rock-collecting there with my dad, and we saw a rattlesnake once. And also a tarantula," I add, even though we really saw the tarantula in Arizona. I don't have any Arizona crystals with me, but I think that big hairy spider should still count for something.

"Did the snake bite you?" Annie Pat Masterson asks, her dark blue eyes wide.

"Almost," I say, like it was nothing—even though in real life, the snake was in the road and I was in the car.

But if I'd gotten out of the car, it could have bitten me.

If it hadn't already been run over.

"Last but not least," I continue, "is the Herkimer diamond, which is fancy quartz, not really a diamond. It's from Herkimer, New York, which is also in the United States." And I hold up something that looks like it might be the biggest diamond in the world. It's almost as large as an orange! Well, a tangerine, anyway.

Stanley Washington's eyes look like they're about to drop out on the floor, he is so impressed.

"Wow," Kevin McKinley says, looking as though he's about to start clapping.

Corey Robinson seems proud just to know me.

"And that's the end of the crystals I brought," I tell everyone, trying to sound modest. "Only these are just six from my dad's collection—which is *huge*."

And when I pick up the crystals and walk back to my chair, my sneakers can't even feel the floor, my whole body is so happy and proud. I feel like a rock star!

"Thank you, EllRay," Ms. Sanchez calls after me. "And I'll be sure to thank Professor Jakes, too, the next time I see him," she adds.

Uh-oh! Ms. Sanchez is very polite. *Too* polite, sometimes.

"No, that's okay," I tell her quickly. "I'll do it for you."

"Now, gather up your things, boys and girls,"

Ms. Sanchez tells everyone after glancing up at the clock. "Because the final buzzer is about to sound. And don't forget to review your spelling words for the test tomorrow—including these two new words: *crystal* and *formation*." And she writes the two words on the board.

I cannot believe something I brought to school will make it onto an official spelling test. *C-r-y-s-t-a-l. F-o-r-m-a-t-i-o-n.*

I just hope I spell those two words right on the test, that's all!

✳ **7** ✳

WHAT AM I SAYING?

Some of the kids in my class crowd around me the very second the final Tuesday afternoon buzzer buzzes—even Jared and Stanley.

This is so cool. My wish has come true! I have never been the most important person in the room before, and it feels *great.*

In fact, I wish this feeling could last forever!

"Can I touch one of the crystals?" Annie Pat asks.

"Sure," I say, because touching a crystal can't hurt it. "Which one?"

"The red one," she tells me. "Red is my new favorite color."

"That's the garnet," I remind her, hauling the lumpy formation out of its sock again.

Annie Pat touches the garnet with her fingertip

as if it might have magical powers. "Um, can I *hold* it?" she asks. "Just for a minute?"

And suddenly, I know how to make this good feeling last a few minutes longer. "You can keep it—"

". . . *for five whole minutes*," I was about to say, but Annie Pat is so excited that she interrupts me.

"Forever?" she asks, like I have just given her a princess crown. She is jumping up and down.

"Sure," I tell her.

What am I saying? That crystal belongs to my father!

"Ooh, what about me?" Cynthia asks, pouncing like a cat going after a grasshopper. "Can I have that baby blue one?"

"It's called a tourmaline," I remind her, my heart crashing around in my skinny chest as I try to think of what to do next. But I can't exactly say no, can I? I mean, I just gave the garnet to Annie Pat!

"And Emma can have the aquamarine crystal," I announce, amazed at my own generosity as I hand over a third crystal.

Three down, three to go. I'm doomed.

"Oh, *thank* you, EllRay," Emma whispers, cradling the blue-green crystal with both hands.

"EllRay?" Ms. Sanchez says quietly, appearing at my elbow as if a genie just rubbed a magic lantern.

"May I have a word with you in private, please?"

"Sure," I say, shrugging to show everyone how not-nervous I am when our teacher asks me this question. I walk over to her desk, where she has been tidying up—and eavesdropping, obviously.

"You're giving your father's crystals away," Ms. Sanchez tells me.

As if I didn't know!

"Well, but it's okay," I lie. "Because my dad said I could. He has lots of them. In fact," I add, "he wants you to have the Herkimer diamond. You can use it for a paperweight or something. But only at home."

"I could never accept such a valuable gift, honey," Ms. Sanchez says.

I hope nobody heard her call me "*honey*," that's for sure.

"It's not a real diamond," I remind her. "But it's way bigger than your engagement ring, so you can see it better. And my father wants you to have it," I repeat.

I sound so sincere!

I hurry to my backpack to get the correct sock.

"He's giving Ms. Sanchez the diamond," I hear some of the remaining kids whisper. They're impressed now, all right! I'll never have to brag again.

"Well, if you're sure," Ms. Sanchez says, her voice still sounding a little doubtful.

"I want the brown one," Kevin says quickly, and so I hand it to him, because—I'm already in so much trouble, why stop now?

And Kevin's my friend, at least.

"I want the gray one," Jared announces, eyeing the last lumpy sock.

And so I hand the smoky quartz crystal to him, almost glad to get it over with. "Sorry, but that's all," I say, showing everyone who's left the six empty socks.

"Aww," a few leftover kids murmer.

"That's no fair," Heather Patton says, scowling.

"Life's not fair," Cynthia tells her, holding onto her tourmaline—*my dad's* tourmaline—as if she is afraid someone is about to snatch it away.

If only I could!

And if only I could turn back the clock—for just ten minutes. Because the wonderful feeling I had five minutes ago has gone. All that's left is the feeling that I am about to yak all over the floor.

What am I gonna tell my dad?

"I hate it when people say life's not fair," Heather says, which is unusual, because usually Heather kisses up to Cynthia like crazy. I almost wish I had another crystal just for her, because I hate that saying, too.

"I need to close up for the day, people," Ms. Sanchez says, standing by the door as she gets ready to turn off the lights. "But don't worry. You'll all be seeing each other in the morning."

We grab our stuff and wander out into the almost-empty hall.

"I'll let you hold my crystal when we get outside," Cynthia promises Heather.

And—it's over.

All except for the part where my dad comes home late tonight.

✳ **8** ✳

DADDY'S HOME!

My dad gets home in five hours, when Alfie and I will already be asleep. I have done everything possible to keep him from noticing that six crystals are missing from his collection.

1. I moved the rest of the crystals again, so now, even though nothing matches its label, there aren't any empty spaces at all left on the shelves.

2. Then I unscrewed the light bulb in the lamp next to the crystal shelves.

3. I even got Alfie to draw Dad a big "Welcome Home" sign before dinner and put it in his office. My dad thinks Alfie's this genius artist, and he might be so happy to see the sign that he won't notice anything in the room is missing.

I can barely even remember this afternoon's good feeling, when everybody liked me, but I think the scared and guilty feeling I have now is probably going to last forever.

And that's another example of something that is not coming out even in my life, in addition to the tallness thing.

"Mom says to tell you dinner's ready," Alfie says, peeking into my room, which she says smells like a hamster cage.

Her daycare has a hamster named Sparky, so Alfie's like this big expert now.

Alfie is golden-brown, and my mom always fixes her soft black hair in three puffy braids: one on top, and one on each side of her head. She has about a million little clip-things to hold the braids shut, and the clips go from fancy to extra-fancy. Even though she is four, she still sucks her thumb when she gets worried or tired.

Everyone always says how cute she is, but don't tell *her* that! She's bad enough already.

"Come *on*, EllWay," Alfie says over her shoulder as I follow her down the hall leading to the stairs. "It's macaroni and cheese night."

We always have dinners with no meat in them when my dad is away, because Mom doesn't like cooking, smelling, or even eating meat too much. And that's fine with Alfie, because all she really likes to eat is cheese—and any dessert under the sun.

But me and my dad love meat. We have a lot in common.

I just hope he remembers that if he ever finds out I gave away those crystals.

"Are your hands clean?" my mom asks Alfie and me as we get ready to sit down. Mom's hair looks extra pretty, and she is wearing fancier clothes than the ones she had on when I got home from school. I guess that's because my dad is coming home. They're still smoochy, but only at home, luckily. I mean, that's bad enough.

"They're *basically* clean," I say, hiding my hands behind my back, just in case. I think I washed them after school, but I can't really remember.

"Mine are basically dooty," Alfie says, which means "*dirty*" in Alfie-speak.

"Go wash," Mom tells Alfie and me. "I'll pour you two some icy cold milk to go with your piping hot macaroni and cheese."

Sometimes Mom sounds like a commercial when she talks about food. It's from being a writer, I guess—or from being hungry.

"Guess what? I'm gonna stay up late, until Daddy gets home," Alfie tells me at the downstairs bathroom sink, sudsing up like she's about to perform an operation on someone. "I'm not even a little bit sleepy," she says, passing me the soap.

"Well, I'm going to bed early," I say. I won't go to bed *right* after dinner, or Mom might think I'm sick. But maybe at ten minutes to eight I can start yawning, and then just melt away into my bedroom so I'll be asleep when Dad gets home.

But from down the hall, I hear an unexpected sound.

The front door is opening.

"Daddy's home!" Alfie yells, throwing Mom's fancy hand towel on the floor and racing out of the bathroom.

"Dad's home," I say quietly, looking at my bug-eyed face in the mirror. "And he's almost five hours **EARLY**. Uh-oh."

"We're so happy you caught that earlier flight," Mom says after the hugging has stopped. "And you're just in time for dinner, but I'm afraid it's only mac and cheese."

"Delicious home cooking," Dad says, smiling. "Let me just get rid of this," he tells Mom, gesturing toward his wheelie bag. "I'll put it in my office for now and unpack after dinner."

"No," I shout, surprising everyone. "I mean, *no*," I say again, more quietly this time. "I'll take it upstairs for you, so you can relax."

"Well, that's very thoughtful of you, son," Dad says. "But dinner's ready. You go ahead and sit down. You can help me later."

"But—"

"Go sit down," Dad says, giving me a puzzled look. "I'll only be a minute."

And so I walk into the dining room with concrete feet— and my dad disappears into his office.

✳ **9** ✳

MISSING

A few minutes later, Dad comes into the dining room with a weird look on his face, just as Mom has finished passing the mac and cheese to Alfie and me.

"What's wrong?" my mom asks, looking up.

"Were there any strangers in the house when I was away, Louise?" he asks. His voice sounds funny, and I start to feel even more nervous.

"Just the electrician," Mom tells him. "Such a nice young man. He came yesterday to give an estimate on adding that new outlet."

"So he went into my office," Dad says, almost to himself.

"Well, yes," Mom replies. "He had to, to see where the outlet was supposed to go. Why? What's wrong?"

"Some things are missing," Dad says quietly.

My mom almost drops the salad bowl, she is so horrified. "Oh, no," she says.

"We had *robbers*?" Alfie squawks, her brown eyes wide. "Maybe they took some of my toys!" And she races out of the room to check.

"I'll calm her down in a minute. What's missing?" Mom asks my dad. "Not your big computer or the printer, I hope."

"No, they're still there," Dad says. "But some of my crystal specimens are gone. It's not that they're so valuable, mind, but they're valuable to *me*. I collected each and every one of them. Whoever took them tried to cover it up, but I noticed right away."

Naturally. Trust eagle-eyed Dr. Warren Jakes not to miss a thing.

"I just can't believe it," Mom says as the salad bowl droops in her hand. "Why, we've used the Bright Ideas Electric Company ever since we moved to Oak Glen. The young man confided to me that this was his first job, too."

"And it'll be his last, if I have anything to say about it," Dad says, scowling. "We're going to have to go through the entire house after dinner, Louise, to see if anything else is missing—before we call the police and fill out the report."

"Oh, no," my mom says, sinking into her chair. "I can't believe that nice young man did such a thing. Maybe this was a one-time mistake, Warren. Can't we simply call the man's boss and ask that he give the crystals back—and anything else he may have taken?"

"We'll do that as well," Dad says, sounding stern. "But Oak Glen doesn't need people waltzing into other people's houses and helping themselves to whatever they like. I'm calling the company *and* the police," he says again.

I feel like I am frozen in my chair as I imagine that I am the electrician who waltzed—I mean walked—into my dad's office yesterday, just trying to do his job. Here is what he could be thinking pretty soon:

1. I studied really hard at Electrician School, and I made it through all the quizzes and tests, even though I got electric shocks, and not the fun kind. I also had to crawl into spiderwebby tunnels and other scary stuff like that.

2. But I finally graduated and was lucky enough to get a good job, and then I went to some nice lady's house to give her an estimate for putting in a new outlet in her husband's office.

3. I liked the lady so much that I even told her this was my first job!

4. Then I got blamed for stealing—even though I never took a thing. And I got fired.

5. *The End.* Of everything.

I **CANNOT** let that happen.

"Wait!" I say to my mom and dad. "Don't call that man's boss. Don't call the police. There's something I have to tell you."

✳ 10 ✳

ULTIMATUM

"Well, what did you *think* was going to happen when I noticed the crystals were gone?" my dad asks after dinner, when we are alone in his office.

I try not to squirm in my chair, but the tiny bit of macaroni and cheese and salad I was able to eat isn't helping any. It is sitting in my stomach like a softball waiting to be pitched. "I didn't get that far," I finally tell my dad. "I guess I just got carried away with being popular for a change."

"*Popular,*" Dad scoffs. He shakes his head in wonder—probably at how dumb the word sounds when I say it.

And that makes me mad, because what kid doesn't want to be popular? Not popular like a TV or rap star, but like a person who other kids admire, at least? So I start talking before I lose my nerve. "You're always saying I should make more friends at Oak Glen," I remind him. "So I just figured—"

"You just figured you'd help yourself to a few of my personal possessions," Dad interrupts, scowling. "That's stealing, EllRay."

STEALING? "No it isn't," I say, my heart thunking so hard in my chest that it's probably bumping into the mac and cheese and salad. "It's not stealing when you borrow something from your own family, Dad," I tell him, hoping this is officially true.

"It's not 'borrowing' when you take something that isn't yours and then give it away," Dad informs me. "And why is it okay to steal from a family member, son?" he asks. "Should you treat someone in your own family worse than you would a stranger?"

"I—I didn't *mean* to give the crystals away," I mumble.

"And I wasn't supposed to find out," Dad says, like he's finishing my sentence for me.

I almost hate my dad right now—because he's making me feel so guilty.

He's probably sorry I'm his son.

"There are lots of aquamarines and topazes in the world," I point out, trying another argument.

"Not ones that I collected when I was in graduate school," Dad snaps. "Not ones I dug out of the earth with my bare hands. I want those crystals back, son."

Now, obviously I am my dad's son. But when he *calls* me "son" like that, it usually means trouble. Not always, but usually.

"I know," I tell him, just for something to say.

"So here's what I'll do," Dad continues. "I'll either call Ms. Sanchez at home tonight and tell her what happened, so that she can make the announcement in class tomorrow morning asking for the prompt return of all six crystals. Or I can come to school with you and make the announcement myself."

"You can't do that," I say, my heart pounding, because—how could I ever live it down? The two friends I have, Kevin and Corey, might never want to talk to me again, I'd look so bad. And so *not honest.*

"I most certainly can," my dad assures me. "But I take it you choose option number one. I'll call Ms. Sanchez this very minute." And he reaches for his cell phone.

Okay. Most parents don't have most teachers' home phone numbers, but it's different at Oak Glen, especially when a kid's behavior *"needs improvement,"* which is what Ms. Sanchez wrote on one of my progress reports a few weeks ago.

Ever since then, it's been Communication City around here.

"Don't call her," I say, jumping to my feet. "Let *me* get the crystals back, Dad. It's my mess, and I should be the one to fix it," I add, knowing suddenly that this is the argument that might actually work with him.

Dad leans back in his swivel chair until it creaks, and he slowly puts down his cell phone on the desk. "Do you think you can do that?" he asks.

"Yes," I say, even though in real life, there is no way I can succeed. But at least it will postpone what is sure to be the most embarrassing moment in my life in eight whole years.

"Fine, then," Dad says. "But here's my ultimatum. Do you know what an ultimatum is?" he asks.

"Not exactly," I admit.

"It's when a person says for the final time that you have to do something, or some consequence will happen," my dad explains. "So listen up. You'll ask for the crystals back tomorrow, Wednesday. But if those crystals aren't in my possession by Thursday evening, I'm marching into your classroom first thing Friday morning, and I'm laying down the law."

"But Friday is Valentine's Day, and that's practically a national patriotic holiday," I remind him, hoping this might buy me another day or two.

Because I do not have a plan for getting back those six crystals.

"Do I look like I care?" Dad asks, obviously not expecting an answer. "I feel certain Ms. Sanchez will back me up on this," he says, softening his tone of voice a little.

"I'll get the crystals back," I say, sounding a lot more sure of myself than I am feeling.

"By Thursday afternoon, or I'm coming in on Friday," Dad reminds me.

"All right," I agree in a shaky voice. "Even though Friday is a very important holiday."

"*Valentine's Day*," my dad says, scoffing once more.

He'd better not let Alfie or my romantic mom hear him say it like that!

But I keep this last thought to myself.

✳ **11** ✳

EMMA AND ANNIE PAT

It is Wednesday, and it is raining hard again, so Mom is driving me to school. Alfie sits next to me in the back seat, and she won't stop yapping.

"Suzette says we're gonna have a Valentine's Day party in day care," she is telling me. "That's in just two more days. Suzette says we're gonna have pink cupcakes. And I'm making Sparky his very own valentine today."

Suzette Monahan came over for a play date once, and she has to be the bossiest four-year-old kid in the world. She even tried to boss my mom around about the snack they were going to have! Suzette is like Cynthia and Jared *combined*, she's such a pain, but Alfie thinks she's great. When they're not fighting, that is.

And like I said before, Sparky is the day-care hamster.

I think he ought to get a medal, not just a valentine!

"I'm putting a hamster-food heart on the card, so he can eat it," Alfie says.

"That's a good idea," I say, staring out the car window at the wet cars, the wet street, the wet sidewalks, the wet *everything*.

This dark and gloomy day matches my mood perfectly, because—how am I going to get my dad's crystals back? I hate even asking someone to lend me an eraser, much less give me back a present I gave them.

In fact, this is a whole new experience for me.

I am beginning to hate new experiences.

"You're not paying attention to me," Alfie complains. "Mom," she calls out, interrupting my mother's important driving concentration. "Make EllWay pay attention!"

"I can't do that, sweetie," Mom says, signaling

to turn left. "But if you say something really, really interesting, I'm sure he *will* pay attention."

This shuts Alfie up for a few blocks. I guess she's trying to think of something awesome to say, so I take advantage of the unusual calm to remind myself of who has which crystal.

1. Annie Pat has the red garnet.

2. Cynthia has the pale blue tourmaline.

3. Emma has the blue-green aquamarine.

4. Kevin has the golden topaz.

5. Jared has the gray smoky quartz.

6. And Ms. Sanchez has the Herkimer diamond, which isn't really a diamond, even though it looks like one and is bigger than her engagement ring. Way bigger.

How am I going to get them back, ever, much less by tomorrow afternoon?

But I have to, or else my dad will march into my classroom on Friday morning and embarrass me more than I've ever been embarrassed in my life!

"We're here," Mom tells me.

"No, wait," Alfie says, grabbing at my sleeve. "I almost thought of something interesting to say."

"Tell me later, after school," I say, flipping the hood of my yellow rain jacket over my head.

"Good luck today, honey," Mom says, catching my eye in her rear-view mirror.

She knows everything, of course. But she loves me anyway.

That's moms for you.

"Thanks," I tell her, opening the car door. "Because I'm gonna need it."

Oak Glen Primary School was built with sunny days in mind, in my opinion, and it's usually sunny in Oak Glen, California. But when it rains, things get a little weird. For example, kids jam together in the hallways before class instead of going out to the playground or the fenced-in yard. And everyone smells wet, and everyone yells.

Then, during nutrition break, we have to eat our snacks in class when it rains—but we can't spill even a crumb, or the mice will come back and Ms. Sanchez will freak again like she did that famous time.

Also, at lunch on a rainy day, everyone has to crowd into the cafeteria instead of eating outside—even the kids who bring their own lunch, like me and most of my friends, because you get to play longer when you bring your lunch.

And during afternoon recess on a rainy day, Ms. Sanchez either plays games with us like "Twenty Questions" or "Simon Says," or, if we "get too squirrelly," as she puts it, she marches us up and down the stairs for exercise with our mouths pretend-zipped shut.

Meanwhile, the real squirrels get to play outside in the rain, and it doesn't do *them* any harm. But nobody thinks of that, do they?

So, basically, rainy days are no fun at Oak Glen, and today, Wednesday, will be the worst one in history. I look around for Kevin or Corey so I will have someone to yell with, at least.

"EllRay," Emma calls out from down the crowded hall, and she and Annie Pat make their way toward me.

"Hi," I say, wondering why Emma wants to talk to me so early. Or at all.

I sneak a look around, but no one is watching, so at least that's okay.

"Thanks again for the aquamarine," she says when she gets to me.

"Yeah," Annie Pat chimes in. "And thanks for the garnet. I showed it to my baby brother Murphy, and he almost tried to eat it, like it was hard red Jell-o. But I didn't let him."

"That's good," I mumble.

"What?"

"*That's good!*" I repeat. "Listen," I say, grabbing

the chance. "I'm really glad you like those crystals and everything, but I gotta get 'em back. It's an emergency," I add, thinking this might make things more convincing.

"What kind of emergency?" Emma asks, her eyes wide. "Are they dangerous?"

"N-n-not exactly," I say slowly, wishing I could say that all the crystals *were* dangerous. Radioactive, maybe, whatever that means. I know it's something bad.

"Well, how come, then?" Annie Pat asks.

She's not mad or anything, she's just asking, and that gives me courage.

"Turns out they were my dad's," I say in a *"Go figure!"* kind of way. Like this was a major surprise to me. "And he decided he needs them back—right away. For important science research reasons," I add, because science is what Emma and Annie Pat like best.

"But I already put mine in my aquarium," Annie Pat says, her red pigtails drooping with disappointment. "So the tetras wouldn't be so bored all day."

Emma frowns, and she plays with a piece of her curly hair. "And I was going to give mine to my mom for Valentine's Day," she tells me.

"She'd probably like a candy bar instead," I say. "A big one. Something chocolate. I'll pay for half of it. And I'll make something else for your fish to look at," I tell Annie Pat, as wet kids push and shove all around us. "Like a LEGO castle, maybe. This is really important, you guys. Can you bring the crystals to school tomorrow?"

"I guess," Annie Pat says sadly, looking as if she would rather not.

"Okay," Emma says. "But we better go, or Ms. Sanchez will yell at us."

Our teacher doesn't yell, but I know what Emma means.

"So let's go," I say, and I cross Emma and Annie Pat off my invisible list of names.

Two down, four to go.

✳ **12** ✳

TICK-TOCK

Kevin McKinley is the opposite of me in every way
except color. Kevin started going to Oak Glen in
kindergarten, and I started in first grade. He's tall,
and I'm short. He's chunky, and I'm skinny. He has
a brother, and I have a sister. He sometimes says
"Present!" when Ms. Sanchez takes attendance,
and Heather Patton usually has to poke me in the
back when our teacher calls my name.

I like to daydream, that's the thing.

But we hang together—with Corey Robinson,
the kid who swims—so I'm not too nervous about
asking Kevin to bring back my dad's topaz. I go up
to him during nutrition break. Nutrition break is
really just morning recess with food, only today,
because of the rain, we're having it in class.

Kevin is over by the window, looking out at the

rain. He keeps dipping his hand into a small crinkly bag of bright orange crackers.

"Hey," I say, unrolling my strawberry fruit leather.

"Hey," he says back, giving me an orange crumb smile.

"I gotta ask you something," I say.

"Okay."

"You know that crystal I gave you? The topaz?" I say.

"Mmm," he nods, chewing.

"I need it back," I say.

"Okay," Kevin says. "I'll see if I can find it in my room."

UH–OH. You should see Kevin's room. I'm surprised he can find his own feet when he gets out of bed in the morning. "I can probably come over this afternoon and help you look for it," I tell him. "I'll call my mom at lunch and ask her."

If kids at Oak Glen have cell phones, which I do not, not yet, they have to leave them in the main office during the day. But there's a pay phone just outside the office, and the lady at the desk will

always lend you the money if you need it. She keeps track, though.

"Okay," Kevin says, smiling, and he reaches into the cracker bag again.

And I cross another name off my invisible list.

Three to go.

✕ ✕ ✕

"Excuse me, Ms. Sanchez?" I ask two seconds after the lunch buzzer has buzzed. "Can I talk to you for a minute?"

Ms. Sanchez tries to hide her sigh. "Of course you *can*, EllRay. You are obviously physically able to speak to me. Are you asking if you *may* speak to me?"

She will never, ever stop correcting us on this one. "*May* I speak to you?"

"You may," she says, sneaking only a tiny peek at her golden watch. "What's up?"

"Well, it's complicated," I say, trying for a thoughtful expression. "But my dad needs that crystal back for his important work. You know, the one I gave you. The Herkimer diamond."

"Ah yes," Ms. Sanchez says with a smile. "That dear Mr. Herkimer."

"Actually, I think Herkimer is a place, not a person," I say, not knowing if she's kidding or not. You can't always tell with teachers, not when they're hungry. "But *anyway*," I repeat, not straying from the topic, "I'm really sorry and everything, but I need that crystal back for my dad's work. Right away, like tomorrow."

Ms. Sanchez narrows her brown eyes and tilts her head, and I can almost feel a question coming. "EllRay," she says slowly, "did you give away those crystals without your father's permission?"

Okay. I could say no, I *did* have his permission, but I know from experience that I'd regret it someday. That lie would come back and bite me.

Also, lying is wrong—but that first reason not to lie is good enough for me.

If I say yes, though, that I *did* give away the crystals without my dad's permission, who knows what will happen?

But if I say nothing at all, I—

"I take it that's a *yes*," Ms. Sanchez says, tapping her foot. "Tick-tock, EllRay."

"*Tick-tock*" means "*hurry up*," when Ms. Sanchez says it.

"Basically," I tell her, looking down at the speckled floor.

"Why did you do it, EllRay?" Ms. Sanchez asks.

Why did I do it? It's funny, I think suddenly—but even my own dad didn't ask me this question. Not exactly. "I don't know," I mumble, still staring at the floor.

"You can do better than that," Ms. Sanchez tells me.

"Well," I say, "I kind of liked it when everyone was paying attention to me in class, for a good reason, I mean, and I wanted them to keep on doing it. And when Annie Pat asked if she could hold the crystal, I just—I got carried away and told her she could keep it."

"Did you *forget* that it belonged to your dad?" Ms. Sanchez asks.

"No," I admit, deciding to keep on telling the truth, because it's the least complicated thing to do, in the long run. "I just wanted the kids to like me a little longer, and giving away those crystals seemed like my only chance."

There is no way she could ever understand about how hard it is for a kid—especially a boy—to be too short to be chosen first for teams, or too bad a speller or mental math guy to win any prizes, or too boring to have an ATV. So I leave those parts out.

"But everyone *already* likes you, EllRay," Ms. Sanchez says, shaking her head in what looks like amazement.

"Not enough."

"Enough for what?" Ms. Sanchez asks. "Did you want to win the popularity contest? Is that it?"

I look up at her. "*Is* there a popularity contest?" I ask, trying not to sound too freaked out. "A real one?"

Don't tell me Cynthia Harbison was right!

"Oh, EllRay," Ms. Sanchez says, shaking her head. "Of course not. But no fear, I'll bring the Herkimer diamond back. You'll have it tomorrow morning. Want me to make an announcement to the class about you needing the other ones returned as well?"

"No, thanks," I say quickly. "I promised my dad that I'd get them back all by myself, by tomorrow. And so far I'm doing okay."

"Tell me if you run into any problems," she says, getting ready to leave. "Is that all?"

"That's all," I tell her. "And thanks, I guess."

"You're welcome, I guess," she says, shooing me out of the room.

So, only two to go.

But they're the worst two: Jared and Cynthia.

✳ 13 ✳

NO WAY, ELLRAY!

I go up to Cynthia right after lunch. She is in the cafeteria, like everyone else on this rainy day, and she is gathering up her very neat trash while Heather waits for her. "I gotta talk to you," I tell Cynthia.

Cynthia looks up, and she looks suspicious. "About what?" she asks.

"About that crystal I gave you yesterday," I tell her. "The tourmaline. I need it back."

Cynthia laughs. "No way, EllRay!" she says.

She looks pretty serious when she tells me this, and Cynthia Harbison is not exactly known for changing her mind about things.

"Yeah," her loyal friend Heather says, glaring at me. "No way. That rock matches her eyes."

"How come you need it back, anyway?" Cynthia asks.

"Because—because I want to give you something even *better* that matches your eyes," I say, making up a fake reason on the spot.

Now, Cynthia looks like she is doing a mental math problem. "Something even better?" she asks, acting a little greedy, if you ask me.

"Like what **KIND** of thing?" Heather says, sounding as if she wants to make sure her best friend doesn't get cheated.

"You know those beautiful blue flowers they have at the supermarket?" Cynthia asks. "The ones that smell spicy and have glitter on the edges of their zig-zaggy petals?"

Flowers? "Uh, yeah. I guess. I'll give you flowers," I mumble, trying to look around like I'm not looking around.

But I sure hope nobody else is listening in on this nightmare conversation.

"Well-l-l," Cynthia says slowly, "if you bring me

those exact flowers on Friday, Valentine's Day, and
you give them to me in front of the whole class, I'll
give you back your blue rock."

"It's a crystal," I remind her. "A tourmaline,
remember? And I need it tomorrow."

"Whatever," Cynthia says, waving her hand in
the air. "I guess I can trust you about bringing me

those flowers. But throw away my trash, while you're at it."

"Yeah," Heather says. "Throw away Cynthia's trash."

"Sorry. That's not part of the deal," I tell them, and I walk away fast—before Cynthia *makes* it part of our deal.

Sparkly blue supermarket flowers!

They sound expensive.

I kiss good-bye all the money I've been saving.

SOMETHING REALLY MESSED-UP

It is still Wednesday, and we are having afternoon recess. It has finally stopped raining, so we are outside. I can tell by the expression on Jared's face that word has gotten out that I need the last crystal back—thanks to Emma, Annie Pat, Kevin, or Cynthia, I guess. But I don't blame any of them for blabbing—because what else is there to talk about at Oak Glen Primary School?

Jared is ready for me when I walk up to him on the rain-shiny playground, which smells like wet chain-link fence, and his friend and robot Stanley Washington is standing next to him. A couple of other kids—including Emma and Annie Pat—are hanging around, too, because it's still too drippy to sit down anywhere. "Dude," Jared says to me, after bouncing the red kickball a couple of times

so hard that it **SPLATS** water on Stanley's pants. "Don't even ask, unless you have something good to give me."

Something good to give him. "Like what, exactly?" I ask, trying to think fast.

Flowers are definitely not gonna do it for Jared, not that I'd ever bring him any.

No way!

"I don't know," Jared says. "Something big. Maybe even money, like—five dollars," he says, obviously making up a number on the spot.

Emma and Annie Pat look wide-eyed at each other when they hear this.

"Five dollars," Stanley says, like he's echoing Jared.

"I thought we were friends," I say, speaking only to Jared—because we *are* friends, at least some of the time. Jared ignored me in both first and second grade, but it's been like being on a roller coaster in the third grade. A mostly uphill roller coaster, if that means Jared has not been a very good friend to me nearly all that time.

In fact, he tried to beat me up once, but that's a different story.

"Five dollars," Jared says again, holding out his hand. "*Now*. Hand it over, EllRay, and I'll bring your rock back tomorrow."

"It's a smoky quartz crystal," I remind him. "And why would I have five whole dollars with me now, in my pocket?" I ask. "You know we aren't allowed to bring that much money to school."

"Okay, then you should make EllRay do some-thing else," Stanley says to Jared, really excited now. "Something *worth* five dollars. Something really messed-up. Like—EllRay should have to go into the girls' bathroom. When there's a girl in it!"

"Classic," Jared says

"Ooh," Emma says, and Annie Pat covers her mouth with her hand, she is so shocked—because it is terrible for a boy to go into the girls' bathroom.

It's probably even against the law!

Also, there aren't just third graders at Oak Glen, there are fourth, fifth, and sixth graders, too. And some of those older girls look pretty tough. They're like grown-ups, practically—and they're *big*.

They could squash me like a **BUG**.

But I need that crystal back.

Behind Jared's back, Emma waves her arms to catch my eye, and she makes an "Okay!" circle sign to me with her thumb and pointer finger.

"Okay," I hear myself say to Jared. "I'll do it. Let's go."

❊ 15 ❊

SCREAMING AND YELLING

"What's the plan?" I whisper to Emma as she and I march across the darkening playground toward the school building.

I don't like having a girl help me, but I'm desperate. I just hope she actually *has* a plan. Emma has been known to get carried away sometimes and promise stuff she can't deliver.

It's because she wants good things to be true, that's the thing.

"Annie Pat ran ahead to empty out the downstairs bathroom," Emma whispers back. "So she'll be the official girl in the girls' bathroom. And I'll stand guard at the door when you go in, so you'll be okay in there. No one will dial 9-1-1 or anything."

"But isn't that cheating?" I ask. "Because Jared wants me—"

"Nuh-uh," Emma interrupts, shaking her head as we scurry along. "It's not cheating. And who cares about what Jared wants? How nice is he being to you?"

Girls care a lot about being nice. Boys care about not getting beat up.

Also, I care about not staying in trouble with my dad.

"There you are," Stanley says in the hall outside the downstairs girls' bathroom. A couple of fifth-grade girls have just hurried out, looking like they are about to gag.

Stanley is almost rubbing his hands together like a cartoon bad guy, he is so happy with his fiendish plan.

"Yeah," Jared says. "Here we are. So let's see you go in there and wash your hands, EllRay! *Slowly*. And then I'll bring that rock back tomorrow."

"It's a crystal," I say again as I stand up straight and get ready to push open the heavy door with the big GIRLS sign on it.

"Whatever, dude," Jared tells me. "Go for it!"

$\times$ $\times$ $\times$

Annie Pat is laughing quietly inside the otherwise empty bathroom. I'm scared even to look around the place, since it is so much against the rules for me to be in here. But I do take a peek.

It looks pretty much the same as the boys' bathroom, only messier. I guess when girls are alone, they're neat. When they're together, watch out!

No wonder our custodian has a bad temper.

"What's so funny?" I ask Annie Pat, my heart pounding so hard I can hear it.

"I told those big girls I was about to barf all over the floor, and they *ran*," she tells me, still giggling. "Now, wash your hands, or at least run the water, and I'll start screaming and yelling so Jared will think he's getting a really good deal out of this. *Eeeee!*" she wails in a high and horrified voice just as I get the water running.

It sounds so real that I turn to stare at her, my heart pounding.

"OUT," she roars, in a different, sixth-grade-sounding voice this time. "This is the *girls'* bath-room, you dummy! Let's get him!"

"Yeah, get him," she says again in a different voice.

Annie Pat should be in the movies or something, she's so good.

I wave my wet hands in the air to shut her up, grab a paper towel to dry my hands, slam-dunk the towel into the trash, and hustle out the bathroom door—into the main hall, where it looks like Emma has just told some little first-grade girls that they have to wait another minute before using the bath-room.

"But I *can't* wait!" one of them is squealing as she jumps up and down in distress. So I hold the door open for her like a gentleman.

"Thanks," she and her friend say, racing into the bathroom.

"He did it," Stanley says, almost looking disap-pointed.

"You did it," Jared says, slapping my hand. "Those girls in the bathroom were really *mad*! It sounded like they were gonna get you good. You got your rock, dude," he adds, heading off down the hall. "Tomorrow."

"It's a *crystal*," I yell after him—even though another rule around here is no yelling in the halls.

But they were right—I did it! And I'll get all six crystals back.

"Congratulations," Emma says, as if she can read my mind.

"Mr. Jakes?" a lady's voice says, and I turn around, my worn-out heart thudding hard once more.

A woman steps out of the doorway opposite the girls' bathroom. I think she's one of the fifth grade teachers, and she's been spying on us. Listening in, anyway.

"Would you care to explain yourself?" she asks. "What on earth were you doing in the girls' bathroom?"

Emma and Annie Pat look like statues, they're so scared. But they don't have to worry. I'm not gonna get them in trouble, too. I owe them.

And even if I didn't owe them, I wouldn't say a word, because—this is my fault.

I started the whole crazy thing when I gave away my dad's crystals.

Just because I wanted something to brag about.

"Cat got your tongue, Mr. Jakes?" the lady asks, staring at me hard, like she really thinks there might be an invisible cat hanging from my mouth.

"I guess," I mumble.

"Hmph," she says, almost snorting. "Well, come

along with me, young man, and we'll see what the principal has to say about this."

The principal!

Not again.

I was only trying to make things right with my dad, and now:

1. I have to make Annie Pat something cool to put in her aquarium so her fish won't be bored.

2. I have to give Emma money for half a candy bar for her mom.

3. I have to wade through all of Kevin's junk after school.

4. And I have to bring Cynthia very expensive-sounding flowers tomorrow, on an official romantic day for girls, and she wants me to give them to her in front of the whole class, which I can't even stand to think about doing.

5. And on top of all that, I'm in trouble with the principal?

I will never look another crystal in the face again for as long as I live!

✳ **16** ✳

OOPS

"Well, Mr. Jakes—so we meet again," the principal says, smiling.

He's actually smiling! I guess he *likes* having kids dragged into his office.

Okay, I wasn't really dragged, but I might as well have been. It's not as if I have a choice about being here.

"Please take a seat," the principal says.

I'm so scared that I forget his actual name. I can spell principal, though, because Ms. Sanchez always reminds us, "The principal is your pal, do you see? The word ends in P-A-L." Like that's a really fun thing. **HAH**.

The principal does try to be nice and say hi to every kid in the morning. He usually calls us "Mister" and "Miss," probably because he thinks that will make us act better.

But I had to go into his office once already this year, and that was one time too many, in my opinion.

And—*do you honestly think my dad's not gonna hear about this?*

"So, EllRay," the principal says, petting the side of his beard. "I hear you strayed into the girls' restroom. What's up with that?"

"I'm sorry. I made a mistake," I say, trying to look him in the eye so he'll think I'm telling him the truth.

"Well, yes, you did make a mistake," he says. "But are you trying to tell me that you didn't realize it was the girls' restroom?"

"That's right," I say, nodding. "I forgot to read the sign on the door."

"And what about all your classmates who were gathered in the hall?" he asks. "High-fiving you and so on. Was that a mistake, too?"

WHOA! Are there spy cameras in the halls, now?

"Let me tell you what *I* think happened," the principal says, not waiting for me to answer his question. "I think it was a dare, Mr. Jakes. I think one of the other boys dared you to go in there, and you took him up on it."

"But nobody in the girls' restroom got embarrassed," I tell him quickly. "We made sure of that."

"We?" he asks, pouncing on the word.

Oops. "I meant '*me*,'" I tell him, because I don't want to get Annie Pat and Emma in trouble, too. Or Jared and Stanley, either. Because what good would that do?

Also, I'd *never* get my dad's smoky quartz crystal back if I told on Jared.

The principal stops petting his beard. He clears his throat. "Ms. Sanchez told me all about the situation with your father's crystals, EllRay," he says.

Whoa. What a squealer she is!

"But why?" I say, and it comes out like a squawk.

"That's between my dad and me, and I'm trying to make it right."

"Glad to hear it," the principal says. "And I applaud you for those efforts, but not when they affect your behavior at Oak Glen."

"I know. I'm sorry," I tell him again.

But really, I'm starting to feel kind of mad.

"Why did you give your father's crystals away?" the principal says.

"Ms. Sanchez already asked me that," I tell him. "I just got a little excited, that's all. I'm only *eight*," I remind him, trying for once to look even smaller than I already am, which is pretty small.

"But what were you hoping to get in return?" the principal asks.

"Respect!" I say, and thunder booms outside.

"You have to earn respect," the principal says. "You can't buy it by carrying out dares or giving away crystals, EllRay."

"But how are you supposed to earn respect when you don't have anything to earn it *with*?" I ask him, my words tumbling out like those little candies in the machine at the supermarket—the machine that always gives you the wrong color candy, as if by magic. "I'm too short to be chosen first in sports," I say, pointing out the obvious. "And I'm not all that great at anything yet except having fun, to tell the truth. So I was trying to use my dad's stuff to get respect, the way everyone else in my class does lately. The boys, anyway. But the whole thing backfired."

"Ah," the principal says.

"I wanted the kids to see how great my dad is," I say. "Even though he'll never buy a humongous TV like Corey's dad or an ATV with flames on it like Jared's dad."

"Some kids do a lot of bragging about their folks in primary school, even these days," the principal agrees. "Just the way some kids do a lot of complaining about them in middle school and high school. But you have to learn to stand alone, Mr. Jakes—and be judged on your own merits."

I don't really know what he's trying to say, so I keep my mouth shut. That is usually the best thing to do at times like these.

Just another hint!

The principal laughs. "You're a good kid, EllRay.

And you—*you*—have a **LOT** to be proud of now."

"Like what?" I mumble, staring down at my sneakers.

"Like, you're a good friend," he says. "For instance, look how loyal you're being to the other kids involved in that restroom caper. And you try to make things right when you mess up. That takes guts."

"I mess up a lot," I admit reluctantly. "So I guess I have lots of guts inside me."

"Everyone makes mistakes," the principal says. "But not everyone takes responsibility for their mistakes the way you do. You're a stand-up guy. I admire you, Mr. Jakes. I think your father is a very lucky man."

I peek at him to see if he is joking. He looks pretty serious, but it's hard to tell with that beard covering so much of his face. "You do?" I finally ask.

He nods. "I do," he tells me. "But I want you to promise me that you'll stay out of the girls' restroom—for at least another week."

Now, he *is* joking. "For the rest of my life," I promise.

"Well, okay then," he says.

"Are you gonna tell my parents?" I ask, looking out the window at the rain.

"Oh," he says, "I think we can keep this between us, don't you?"

And I nod yes, of course, because I really, really think we can.

Really.

✳ 17 ✳

VALENTINE'S DAY

My mom is amazed when I say we have to leave early for school today because I need her to drive me to the supermarket. "Why?" she asks.

"I gotta buy something," I mumble. "With my saved-up allowance and Christmas money."

Alfie is listening in, naturally.

"Lancelot Raymond Jakes," my mom says, frowning. "Don't you dare tell me I was supposed to make cupcakes for that party today."

"We get to have cupcakes too, at my day care, 'cause it's Valentine's Day," Alfie says, almost drooling at the breakfast table. "Pink, with chocolate sprinkles, I hope."

"It's not cupcakes," I tell Mom. "It's flowers. I have to buy this special kind of flowers for someone."

"Oh, *EllRay*," my mom says, her brown eyes

shining with romance and other embarrassing things. "Of course I can take you to the store. Who are the flowers for, honey? Or is it a great big secret?"

"Are they for me?" Alfie asks, frowning. "Because I like candy best, not toopid flowers."

"They're for someone at school, okay?" I say, thinking that Cynthia would be really happy to see me suffering so much just because of her—and because of that tourmaline, which she handed over first thing yesterday morning.

I'll give her that much credit.

"I know. They're for Ms. Sanchez," my mom says like she has solved a riddle. She sounds thrilled. "Well, I think that's just about the sweetest thing I ever heard."

"They're not for Ms. Sanchez," I say, trying not to yell.

"Then they're for **SOME GIRL,**" Alfie exclaims. "Ooo," she says, and she starts kissing the back of her hand again and again.

"EllRay," Mom says, astonished. "Really?"

"Don't get all excited," I tell her gloomily. "It's not what you think."

But I can't tell her I'm bringing flowers to school because I'm basically being blackmailed, can I? She'd get even *more* excited, then. And not in a good way.

My dad walks into the kitchen like he's going someplace important, and he kisses my mom and pours himself a cup of coffee. "Today's the day," he says.

As if any of us needed reminding.

"It certainly is, Warren," my mom says, and she instantly changes his mood by putting his coffee cup on the counter, then whirling him around the kitchen in a pretend dance.

"Me too!" Alfie cries, trying to jam herself between them.

"I'm gonna just go brush my teeth," I tell everyone, but I don't think they hear me.

✕ ✕ ✕

"Good morning, ladies and gentlemen," Ms. Sanchez says above the excited, special-day buzz everyone is making. "And happy Valentine's Day!"

The girls are all dressed up, of course, but the boys just look normal.

All except me, because I'm the kid who's holding a drippy bunch of blue flowers in his lap. And now there's glitter all over my pants. I'll probably sparkle all day long.

Thanks a lot, Cynthia.

"As you know," Ms. Sanchez says, "we won't be opening our valentines until the end of class, when we'll also be having a little party, thanks to our wonderful parent volunteers. But it looks as though EllRay has a special valentine that just can't wait. EllRay?" she says, sounding both encouraging and ready to thank me.

She thinks the flowers are for her.

And so does everyone else. *Almost* everyone.

Cynthia and Heather are grinning like crazy, of course.

Well, I might as well get this over with. I walk to the front of the class. "These are for—for Cynthia Harbison," I say, forcing myself to say her name, and I **SQUINCH** my eyes shut like a bolt of lightning is about to strike me down right here in front of Ms. Sanchez and her third grade class. "Happy Valentine's Day, Cynthia," I manage to add, in case Cynthia thinks that's part of the deal.

Ms. Sanchez—and most of the other kids—look totally stunned.

"For *me*?" Cynthia squeals, gasping to show how surprised she is, and she races to the front of the class like she's got little jet engines in her shoes.

What a faker!

"Take 'em," I mutter, and she does.

"Oh, thanks," she exclaims, and head down, I hurry back to my seat before she even *thinks* of hugging or kissing me, in case that was part of her terrible plan. "I don't know what to say," Cynthia continues, looking as though she's about to start saying a *lot*. It's as if she's just won a huge award or something.

"You don't need to say a thing," Ms. Sanchez tells her briskly. "Please take your seat, and we'll put those flowers in some water right after I finish taking attendance."

I think Ms. Sanchez knows exactly what happened.

I just hope the other kids do, too. Especially the boys.

"Okay," Cynthia says, looking sorry that she can't drag out her minute of glory a little longer. "Ohh," she says, sniffing the flowers noisily as she goes back to her seat.

I hope she gets glitter up her nose!

"Dude," Kevin whispers to me, looking confused and disappointed. "Dude."

"I'll tell you later," I whisper back.

✻ **18** ✻

PROUD

"That was some fancy bunch of flowers you gave Cynthia this morning," Ms. Sanchez says that afternoon at the Valentine's Day party, after taking a dainty nibble of her pink-frosted cupcake.

We also have pink lemonade to drink. This is a very girly celebration, in my opinion, but the food's good if you close your eyes and forget about the color.

"I assume it was a trade?" Ms. Sanchez asks. "For her crystal?"

I take a huge bite of my cupcake, because I can't figure out whether or not this is a trick question. Will I get in trouble again if I answer it? Or if I *don't* answer it? Or will I get Cynthia in trouble?

Sometimes it's tough being me!

"I dunno," I finally say, hoping I don't have a

dab of frosting on my nose—the way Cynthia does.
SCORE.

She just went prancing by holding her flowers.

"And can I assume a few lessons have been learned?" Ms. Sanchez asks, but she sounds more jokey than strict.

So I get up enough nerve to say, "Excuse me, but do you mean *are you physically able* to assume that?" Just to tease her.

Maybe it's the sugar, like my mom's always saying.

"Point taken, Mr. Jakes," Ms. Sanchez says, laughing. "*May* I assume a few lessons have been learned?"

"You may," I say, eyeing the few leftover cupcakes on the long table.

"You're something else, do you know that?" she tells me, still smiling.

And however she means what she just said, I decide to take it as a compliment. "Thanks," I say, smiling back at her. "You too. Happy Valentine's Day, Ms. Sanchez."

It is now Friday night, and my mom and my dad—who counted and inspected every crystal yesterday, and then shook my hand and actually hugged me tight—are busy getting ready to go out for dinner. Mom made a special dinner for Alfie and me. She even got two DVDs for us to chose from, with Monique, our sitter, acting as referee.

Monique's okay. She knows how to crack her knuckles and dance.

I just put Alfie's "required valentine" on her dinner plate, and I'm pretty sure she'll like it.

1. Her valentine is at least four times as big as the one I made for Mom.

2. It shows two fuzzy kittens sitting in a basket, and Alfie loves kittens, big surprise.

3. And there is paper lace all around the edges.

4. Also, I used silver duct tape to stick two candy bars onto it!

Alfie comes sneaking into the kitchen with her hands behind her back. "Happy Valentine's Day, EllWay," she says, mispronouncing my name as usual. And then she hands me something.

It's a crystal!

A purple amethyst.

"But *shhh*. Don't tell Daddy," she whispers. "I went into his office and took it. But he's got tons, so that's all wight."

"Alfie," I say, "it's *not* all wight. I mean, all *right*. We gotta put this back fast!"

If Dad gets mad again, he might cancel our secret shopping trip tomorrow. The one for the spray paint, where I get to choose the colors.

Yellow, orange, and purple, by the way.

"I don't want to," she says, her face puckering up the way it does when she's about to cry. "It's your *valentine*."

"This crystal is Dad's private property," I tell my little sister, trying to keep my voice quiet. "But it's the thought that counts," I say quickly, and she cheers up pretty fast. "Thanks, Alfie. Now, let's go."

And we tiptoe down the hall toward Dad's office and put the crystal back on his display shelf, then we creep back toward the kitchen like bad guys on a TV crime show.

"Where's *my* valentine?" Alfie asks when we get back to the kitchen. And then she spots it. "Yay-y-y!" she shouts, clasping the big lumpy card to her chest. "And it's got candy bars on it! My favorite kinds, too!"

"I hope you like it," I tell her, trying to sound modest.

Actually, I hope she'll *share*, but I'm not exactly holding my breath.

Mom and Dad bustle into the room just as there's a knock on the door. "Well, isn't that nice of your big brother," Dad says to Alfie about the big valentine, while Mom goes to greet the sitter. "Good job, son. I'm proud of you. For a whole lot of reasons," he adds, giving me a special look.

"You are?" I ask, suddenly feeling kind of shy. Shy, around my own dad!

"I am," he says, nodding his head.

"And me too, Daddy?" Alfie says, horning in as usual.

"You too, baby girl," he says, nuzzling her neck.

But he shoots me another special look, and I feel really good.

"Now, you children behave," my mom tells Alfie and me as they get ready to go out the door for their probably-smoochy dinner. "And you mind Monique, hear?"

"Okay, Mommy," Alfie says, giving Mom a final hug.

"Okay," I say too, and I sound a lot more confident than I usually do when I make this babysitter promise.

But I'm not gonna go getting in trouble again. Not so close to last time.

NO WAY!

DON'T MISS

EllRay Jakes
is <u>NOT</u> a chicken!

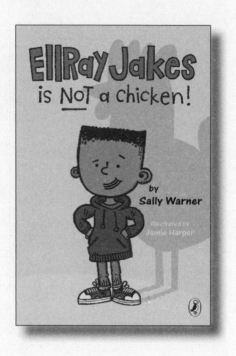

The first book featuring EllRay
by Sally Warner and Jamie Harper